999 TIPS TO MAKE EVERY MAN
FALL IN LOVE WITH YOU
AND EVERY WOMAN ENVY YOU

HOW
TO
BE A
SUPER
HOT
WOMAN

MANDY SIMONS
EMILY J. TERRY

Outskirts Press, Inc.
Denver, Colorado

D0088455

Outskirts Press
http://www.outskirtspress.com

ISBN-10: 1-4327-0392-7
ISBN-13: 978-1-4327-0392-9

Outskirts Press and the "OP" logo are trademarks belonging to
Outskirts Press, Inc.

Printed in the United States of America

TABLE OF CONTENTS

MAKE UP AND CLOTHING TIPS

1. Dress in colorful clothes. They make you look fresh and bright. They bring positive mood, joy and happiness to all people around you.

2. Wear high-heeled shoes. They are always modern and make your legs look irresistibly desirable. Men adore high heel shoes and find them very sexy.

3. Hair is one of the first things that make impression in a person. Keep it in good health and clean. Use good hair products and vitamins that will make her vital and sparkling.

4. Don't buy clothes only because they are from famous designers. They may be very expensive and top fashionable but that doesn't mean that they will look good on you. Appraise what will fit you most. No matter if it is cheap or expensive. The most important thing is to suit you. Just because it's the latest fad doesn't mean it'll look good on you. Learn to choose clothes that flatter your figure, and not just because it's the hottest style. If

you must, try to select a variant of the style that will work best for you.

5. Keep your hair long. Or if it is short let it grow. Men like women with very long hair. You can be blonde, brunette or with red hair. No matter what the color or the style of your hair is, it should be long.

6. If your hair is short and you can't wait for it to grow long, start using hair extensions. Your hair will not only become longer but it also will be thicker. The effect is outstanding. Your hair will look very beautiful and no one will know you wear hair extensions unless you tell them.

7. Use make-up every day. There is no such thing as naturally beautiful woman. Men always prefer women who use make-up to highlight their beauty.

8. Always use complexion as a base make-up. It will cover and hide all your spots on your face and will make it smooth with velvety feel.

9. Lip gloss is a must. Take light or dark pink gloss. When you use it your lips will look very juicy and tempting and every man will want to taste them with a kiss.

10. The black mascara highlights your beautiful eyes.

It's another important element which you must use. Without it the make-up on your face will look incomplete.

11. If you don't want your face to look oily by-mid-day, use powdered mineral makeup instead of liquid or cream makeup. The layers of powder seem to stay put better and they deter shine.

12. You can give your skin an extra glow by using facial scrub. Made with ingredients like almond or walnut shells, oatmeal or cornmeal, facial scrubs exfoliate the skin, scraping off the dead cells and leaving fresh ones gleaming.

13. Use hand lotions. Hand lotions can do more than keep your hands soft- if you have sensitive or overworked skin, the right lotion can heal the little cuts and crack that can make your hands hurt.

14. Eyebrows are tricky and should only be colored by a professional in a salon. Bleaching eyebrows is risky if you try it alone, because even a single drip, if it falls into your eye, can cause blindness.

15. You must smell like a flower. You should find a fragrance that suits you by starting with what you love. Perfume shopping is a big fun, but you have to be prepared for it.

16. You can make your perfume last longer. Layer

your perfume with a lotion of the same fragrance. Don't rub your wrists together after spraying on perfume. It actually damages the chemical composition of the perfume and causes the fragrance to break down quicker. Buy the more expensive eau de parfume over the eau de toliete version. The parfume will have a higher concentration of fragrance helping the smell to last longer and this is why it cost a little bit more. A bottle of perfume really only lasts for 12-24 months. If you have had your bottle of perfume longer than that you should replace it for the intended fragrance affect.

17. Brush your teeth with baking soda and peroxide instead of a regular toothpaste. This is the most practical and effective home tooth whitening system found so far.

18. You can keep your nails strong and prevent breaking. Don't use your nails as tools, which will only weaken their structure. Don't bite your nails and cuticles, which can damage nail beds and a healthy growing cycle. Wear rubber gloves while doing dishes, household cleaning anytime your nails will be in contact with soap or water or other cleaning chemicals for extended periods of time. The chemicals and soap can weaken nails. Don't use nail polish remover more than twice a month. The chemical in the remover can have a weakening affect on nails. Don't forget to moisturizer. Just

like your skin and hair needs moisture, so do your nails. Massage lotion into your nails and cuticles each day when you apply lotion to your hands.

19. There is a quick technique for applying makeup. The basic steps are to apply a light foundation or tinted moisturizer with a cosmetic sponge to even out your skin complexion. Brush on some blush to the apples of your cheeks and apply a sheer lip gloss to your lips. Lastly, sweep on 1-2 coat of mascara to your lashes and you're done! Once you get the hang of the routine it actually takes less than five minutes.

20. You can make your thin lips look fuller by outlining them ever so slightly in a subtle but definite wear proof lip liner, then will in with lipstick. Apply a little pearls cent or shimmer lipstick or gloss in the middle of your lips after the full coat of lipstick.

21. You can do a proper French manicure at home. You need a base coat in a neutral sort of peach, pinky-translucent or clear polish, a bottle of white polish for the tips and some sticky nail tip guides to keep your polish tidy.

22. There are signs that you are wearing too much makeup: you scratch your skin and end up with a fingernail full of foundation, friends don't recognize you when you are au naturel, when you

wipe your mouth at lunch, and you are left with a streak of base and lipstick on your napkin.

23.   Very dark lip liner only works if you're wearing very dark lipstick. Otherwise, it leaves you with obvious ring-around-the-lips. It also accentuates fine lines around the mouth. Invest in neutral-colored pencil that works with all lipstick shades.

24.   There are pencil eyeliners, liquid eyeliner, and cake eyeliners. Pencil liners can be used above top lashes and under lower lashes. Liquid liners should only be used on the top lid. Cake eyeliners are used with water and can be used both top and bottom.

25.   To achieve the look of dark, dramatic eyes, use a kohl pencil to outline top and bottom lashes and follow with a black liquid liner to the top lashes only.

26.   Brown eyes look great in blues and pink tones as well as gold and burnt oranges. The intensity of color you wear depends on your skin tone. For fair skin, use a soft blue on the eyelid, plum on the outer edge of the eye, and pink under the eyebrow. For medium to deeper skin tone, the plum could be used on the lid and into the crease area. Line eyes with a navy or plum color and black mascara.

27.   For blue eyes and blonde hair the best looking eye

shadow colors are violets and lavenders or neutral tones. Use the violet on the lid and in the crease of the eyelid. Use the lighter color lavender above the crease to the eyebrow bone for a dramatic night look. Use natural colors for daytime.

28.   There are some mascara mistakes to avoid: do not wear colored mascara such as a blue, purple or green if you're going for a professional daytime look, do not wear a mascara that smears, do not use waterproof mascara on a daily basis because they are difficult to remove and too hard on your lashes, do not forget to apply mascara evenly to lower lashes, do not over apply mascara, because your lashes will look clumpy.

29.   Blush can be almost every color as long as it coordinates with the lipstick color, but it must be blended softly, without any noticeable edges.

30.   Powder should match the foundation exactly or go on translucent so as not to affect the color of the foundation.

31.   If you are wearing wardrobe colors like red or pink you can match the lipstick with that color. However, try not to clash color tone. For example, if the outfit you are wearing is peach or coral, your blush and lipstick should have the same underlying color or be a neutral tone.

32.   To create a tanned appearance, use golden brown

and chestnut shades for your blush, eyeshadows, contour, and lipstick, but do not, under any circumstances, apply a foundation or bronzer all over the face if it leaves a line of demarcation at the jaw or hairline.

33.   To prevent your lips from feeling dry when you apply matte lipstick, apply lip balm on your lips before start your make up. By the time you do your eyes and the rest of the face your lips would have absorbed the balm and will be ready for the matte lipstick.

34.   To fix unpolished nails, fail nails into square shape, buff them to give some shine and then apply a clear coat of polish. Then rub a little cuticle oil around the edges of your nails and apply rich moisturizer on your hand. In about 15 minutes your hand will have a polished look.

35.   Lipstick staining your teeth makes you look extremely shabby. To avoid this, pucker your lips in an extreme 'O' and then apply the lipstick.

36.   If the upper lip is too thin or does not have a good shape, outline it with the lip liner similar to your lipstick and in the center portion, draw a second line giving it the precise shape using a brown pencil. Apply color including the brown line. This will make your lips look fuller.

37.   Removing your make up is essential for

maintaining a good complexion. Pull your hair away from your face. Using water and water soluble cleanser gently wash the eye make up off. Try not to pull on this gentle area. Excessive pulling can cause the skin to sag. If you are using waterproof mascara, you might want to use a wipe-off make up remover. Choose a skin cleanser that is appropriate for your skin type. There are numerous products on the market which are especially made for dry, normal, or oily skin. If you use heavy foundations, you may want to use a wash cloth to clean your skin. For delicate skin, avoid using a cloth as it might be too harsh. If you are not using a cloth, use your fingers to gently spread the cleanser around your face. Use tepid water. Water that is too hot or too cold can be irritating to the skin. Rinse the cleanser thoroughly. You don't want to leave behind a soapy residue. Pat dry with a soft towel. Follow with a moisturizing night cream if that is part of your beauty routine.

38.   Blouses: a collared shirt always gives a torso a few good inches and frames the face handsomely.

39.   Show off the trimmest parts of your body by combining a tight fitting piece with a loose fitting one.

40.   There is never an excuse for panty lines. A thong is a girl's best friend - they even come with

tummy control.

41.   Don't worry if separates don't match exactly. Tonal variations are a creative alternative.

42.   The darker a print's background, the slimmer the look.

43.   Any color worn head to toe in a clean, unbroken line will produce a dynamically slimming effect.

44.   Taller bodies can take larger prints and more contrast.

45.   A slim v-neck makes the neck appear longer and is usually very flattering.

46.   If your legs are fuller inside, try a side slit. If your legs are fuller outside, a mid-front or back slit is a better choice.

47.   Stilettos are back and in spite of the discomfort at times - they make your legs look like a million dollars.

48.   A shoulder bag tucked quietly under the arm is most flattering.

49.   Tall women: can indulge in wide belts, should avoid skirts that are too short or too long, can tuck shirts into pants and skirts to create a horizontal

line to show off their waist line, can wear horizontal patterns and textured fabrics, can wear longer or flared skirts, can wear short skirts, especially when paired with knee-high boots.

50. Petite women: horizontal lines cut off the figure and make us appear wider and shorter than we are. Avoid tops and bottoms that are in high contrast colors (a white top and black pants, for example). It is better to choose similar colors to create an elongated look, Vertical lines such as pleats, v-necklines, open jackets and slacks create an elongated silhouette, the same color (monochromatic) from head to toe will also create a continuous, lengthwise flow. Blend similar colored shoes and hose to appear taller, avoid tops that hit below mid-high unless paired with a skirt that falls above the knee.

51. Plus size women: Choose monochromatic outfits, with tops and bottoms in the same color; to elongate the body, wear opaque hose that match your skirt, stay away from chokers and opt for long necklaces to make the neck seem elongated, draw attention to shapely shoulders with boat neck tops and styles that go slightly off the shoulder, avoid shoes with heavy buckles, bows or T-straps, because they create a widening effect, flare-bottom pants or jeans create the illusion of narrower hips, a gently pointed toe is more flattering than a round or square toe, skirt hems should extend over your

boots to create vertical length, stay away from handbags that are tiny or too dainty, as they will not complement your voluptuous figure, although ankle boots are always a safe bet, if it's a knee-length boot you seek, be sure they it's made with the plus-size calf in mind.

52.   Just because a pair of jeans looks great on your same-size friend doesn't mean they are right for you. Like with any piece of clothing, you really need to try jeans on to see how they work. If you have curvy hips and are proud of them, super-low boot-cut jean are good, which sits well on the hips and shows off your figure. Women who want a little room in the thighs and calves should look at styles that don't hug the body, such as relaxed fit or boy-cut jeans. And for extra room in the seat, try jeans with a low waist, low pockets and a bit of a flare around the ankle.

53.   Style is the way you put together clothes, not the clothes themselves. There is something to be said for picking clothes you won't get sick of but that feel good. Unless you don't mind getting rid of certain items every season, stay away from overly trendy pieces when shopping for your basic wardrobe. Don't pick everything you see in magazines. Pick what looks and feels better on you. This comes with being honest and true to yourself. Wear what's right for your body type and don't be a slave to fashion. Your wardrobe should show your personality, not

the personality of the store's salesperson.

54.   If you want to look sporty: wear layered coordinates always pulled together with a vest, blazer, or anorak style jacket. Head Gear like baseball caps can give many just casual outfits that sporty feel.

55.   If you want to look freestyle: arty, funky style always with a twist. You will try the latest trend but adapt it for your figure. You love hats and look terrific in them.

56.   If you want to look elegant/classic: your clothes never enter the room before you do. You are known for clothes in the best fabrics, simple style, one good piece of jewelry, genuine leather accessories.

57.   If you want to look sexy: you enjoy clothes that enhance your curves-fluid fabrics, deeper necklines, waist treatments, sensual fabrics like silk, cashmere, slinky knits and leather.

58.   If you want to look romantic: you love being a woman and enjoy lace touches, soft floral and peals.

59.   Dry brushing your skin before a shower is a great way to stimulate the natural oil glands in your body. Using a natural bristle body brush, start at

your feet and lightly "brush" your skin in a circular motion. Follow by a warm shower and slather your body with your favourite moisturizer.

60.   Dip into your fridge for facial cleansers when your regular cleanser runs out. In a pinch buttermilk, yogurt and even cream are gentle, natural skin cleansers.

61.   Instead of using a cream moisturizer after you bath or shower, rub almond oil into your skin for a treat. Combined with a few drops of your favourite essential oil (peppermint, lavender or neroli) it will leave your skin smooth and supple.

62.   An easy way to avoid razor burn after shaving is to moisturize beforehand. While shaving cream is the most popular method, try prepping your leg with hair conditioner for a few minutes before shaving. It will hold moisture on the leg longer and provide a very smooth shave.

63.   Need to get rid of tired or puffy eyes immediately? Keep a spoon in the freezer and apply to eyelids for a few minutes to reduce redness.

64.   Hair sets best as it is cooling, not when it is heated up from blow-drying. Whether using hot rollers or a blow dryer, apply hair spray after hair has cooled to maximize the style.

65. Separate your damp hair into several sections and blow-dry one at a time using a round or paddle brush. Taking the time to focus on each section will give you that overall salon look.

66. To ensure your eyes stay healthy and free of infection when using make-up, heed the following due-date rules. Throw out your mascara after three months, powder eye shadows every nine to 18 months, and cream eye shadows every six to 12 months. Sharpen your eyeliners often to keep them clean.

67. Pamper your tired feet with a luxurious footbath. Fill a basin with warm water and add a few drops of essential oils. Next place marbles or small stones (found at your local garden centre) into the basin. Run your toes and soles of your feet over the marbles, and relax for 15 minutes.

68. Before sharpening your eyeliner or lip pencil, place them in the freezer for 10 minutes. They will harden slightly and not break when sharpened.

69. Apply foundation to your face after you have done your eye make-up. This helps you to fix any last minute smudging from mascara or eyeliner under the eyes.

70. Apply a lip balm to lips before starting your

make-up routine. By the time you have done your eyes and rest of the face, your lips will be moisturized and ready for the matte lipstick.

71.   If you have been sloppy applying nail polish, simply soak nails (when dry) in warm water for a few minutes and then rub off extra nail polish gently with a finger.

72.   Many women suffer from unwanted facial hair. Often facial hair in women appears first during puberty and then becomes more prolific from the age of 35 +. Use laser hair removal - By far the best method, producing relatively fast permanent results with 6 - 8 sessions, the only downside is the price.

BEST WARDROBE WITHOUT SPENDING MUCH TIPS

73. Every woman dreams of wardrobe full of the latest fashion that all the celebrities wear. Never fear, you don't have to be reach to do this. Look for sales, like 75% off. These are rare but they have expensive designer wear for less than half the price.

74. All women want designer bags that celebrities wear. You don't need to sell your grandma for them. Shop online. You can get fake ones for 75% off the retail price.

75. Spend big on: coats, jackets, little black dress, jeans and denim skirt. Don't spend big on trend pieces- celebs tend to mix and match designers with cheap items. Don't buy clothing that is too tight. It looks tacky, is uncomfortable and can send the wrong message to co-workers and/or peers.

SELF-ESTEEM TIPS

76. Believe in yourself. For every negative belief you hold about yourself think of four positive ones. If you can't think of beliefs that are true at the moment then think of beliefs you would like to be true that you can work towards.

77. Choose two things that you know you are good at and think of three ways you could work to improve each of these even more. By concentrating on areas that you know you are already good at will improve your confidence and be a good building block for future success.

78. It's easy to feel self-conscious if you have nothing to do, and much more difficult if your attention is occupied by a task. Think how comfortable you have been with others when you're all working toward a common goal. The common goal of socialising could be making friends, it could be the exchange of mutually

beneficial information, it could be whatever you want it to be.

79.   Speaking positively, whether of yourself or over your life will affect how you feel and even how others view you. Even if you have a bad day, or make a dumb mistake – remember you're only human.

80.   Being happy in your own skin means getting comfortable with who you are, the way you look and what you want out of life. Instead of focusing on what you don't like about yourself, do your best to honour and appreciate what makes you unique. Your smile. Your sense of humour. Do you have wonderful hair or fabulous cheekbones? Now go further. What qualities define you as a person? What do you absolutely love about yourself? Is it your attitude?

81.   Never compare yourself with others. This is the easiest way to feel inferior and lose self-esteem. It is much better to rate yourself on your achievements. Such an approach will give you self-confidence. At the same time it will make you feel better when dealing with your peer group.

82.   Always be positive about yourself and keep reminding yourself about your good qualities, your accomplishments and how you help your family, friends, others and yourself. Don't make the

mistake of brooding over negative things, and never put yourself down.

83.   It's normal to cry when experience a pain. But don't let pain transform itself into fear. Forget about it and move on. Life is great and there will be great moment for you. Treat each failure and mistake as a lesson.

84.   Never put yourself down. As mentioned before, failures are experiences to learn from and move forward, but give them too much attention and they will eat away your self-confidence, self-respect and self-esteem. Keep positive thoughts in your mind if you want others to treat you with respect. People will respect when you project a positive exterior, even in the most adverse situations. Make it a small goal to filter out all self-criticism.

85.   Take care of your body. Self-esteem is also dependent upon the feeling of well-being. Someone who takes care of their body will be a more confident individual than someone who is lazy and poorly groomed. Remember, a healthy body is essential for a healthy mind.

86.   Believe in yourself and your ability to accomplish things. Believe that you have the power to control your life.

87.   Associate with positive people. Think positively and speak positively.

88.   Know your strengths and weaknesses. Know your limitations. Expect yourself to be the best you can be.

89.   Be happy and satisfied with yourself and your personal life. Be happy and satisfied with your work life.

90.   Take risks that you feel comfortable with, and then expand your boundaries. Do good and nice things for you, things that make you feel good about yourself.

91.   Love yourself and your family. Tell yourself every day that you have a high level of self esteem, and then go out and do things that support this affirmation.

BE THANKFUL TIPS

92.   If you take your life for granted then you should
        change. If you want to live happy you should be
        thankful for everything. Look around and pay
        attention to the people around you. You will find
        that everybody has something to worry or
        complain about, not just you. Even rich people
        might look happy but you never know what's going
        on inside. They might be miserable as well. Look
        at those who aren't as fortunate as you are and
        count your blessings.

93.   Stop worrying on how things should be, what
        could've been, and what you don't have. Be glad
        what you have and appreciate it. Accepting your
        lot in life is not about resigning yourself to
        unhappiness.

94.   Get in the habit of asking yourself how you can
        turn the negative into a positive. Be happy and
        enjoy every second of your life. Let the small

things make you happy. Enjoy your family, friends, job, flowers, dog, etc.

95. Imagine yourself looking back ten years from now. Be proud how much you have succeed. You have coped with all the difficult circumstances. So be proud of yourself and respect more yourself.

96. Life's treasures are the small pleasures. Give thanks for each small gift you receive. No matter how positive and thankful you are, remember that life will always have its ups and downs. You're going to have to take the good with the bad.

STAY POSITIVE TIPS

97.   All people have some nice qualities. Have you
        ever thought about your best qualities? May be you
        are funny or pretty? Or may be you are such a
        great businesswoman? Or very good-natured?
        Write down on a paper your qualities, read them
        several times until you feel the power of yourself.
        Be proud of yourself.

98.   Remove the negative thoughts forever. Often,
        people say, "I am fat" or "I am stupid", or "no one
        loves me". Prove to yourself that you aren't this
        and that. If you think you're fat, look at everyone
        else in your age group, you're probably among the
        middle. Find some beautiful things about
        yourself...do you have nice skin? Long nails?
        Pretty eyes? Full lips? Find stuff that appeals to
        you.

99.   Determine what you want to change in your life.
        What will make you feel better? Make a few goals

and try to find ways to get there. There is always a way out of your problems. Go for your goals, never give up and achieve them.

100. Keep you motivation in order to reach your goals. What gives you energy to go on everyday? Family? Children? Music? Love? Job? Friends? Yourself? Keep thinking of those for motivation. Go for what you want.

101. Remember that this is only one part of your entire life. Remember that the sun will shine again for you. You will be again happy with great moments. May be this will be tomorrow, may be next week or may be next month, but you will feel better.

SMILE TIPS

102. Always brush your teeth in the morning before breakfast. You will have sweet breath and your teeth will be bright and clean.

103. It's not easy but you should stop worry about things that you can not change. You can not change the past either so stop thinking about this and think happy thoughts. If you only worry lines will appear on your face and you will accomplish nothing.

104. If you think about negative thoughts, you won't be able to smile. Enjoy the small things in your life, your family, job, friends, clothes, whatever you want. When you are happy inside, you will automatically have a smile on your face.

It's not bad also to pretend to smile because when you pretend it can eventually lead you to a good mood. So keep smiling! Smiling to another person, will cause that other person to smile as well.

105. It's very important to get plenty of sleep because without it you won't be able to smile. You can make your fake smile look more realistic by raising your eyebrows.

106. There is a saying "Frown and you frown alone, but smile and the whole world smiles with you". You can practice a great smile. Stand in front of the mirror and just smile. Change your thoughts each time, and see how your thoughts reflect the type of smile that others see.

SPORT TIPS

107. Work up to exercising at least 30 to 45 minutes per day 4 or 5 days per week. Depending on your level of fitness, you may want to work up to that gradually. Exercising four times a week is more than enough to maintain a good level of fitness.

108. Spend most of your time on aerobic exercises. You can burn many calories doing aerobic exercises. Do include strength training exercise as well. Lesser amounts of exercise are adequate if your goal is longevity or a healthy body and mind. If your goal is to lose weight, you need to work towards exercising most days.

109. There are three exercises that make a complete workout. The first is flexibility exercise, which includes stretching and loosening the body and muscles. The next is endurance exercise such as jogging or swimming. The third type of exercise is strength exercise; it involves weightlifting and

body work. These three exercises don't need fancy equipment so they are inexpenisve.

110. You can do exercises while watching TV. Make a habit of exercising during commercials but never eat while watching TV. Keep the volume on if you find yourself constantly looking to see if the commercials are over. Stretch for a short time when the commercials are over.

111. Fitness improves as exercise becomes more frequent. It also slows the process of aging. The advantages of having good health and fitness are well worth the time and energy they require.

LOOK SKINNIER TIPS

112. Buy clothes that fit you. Wear clothes that are not too tight and not too big. Wearing clothes that are too tight leads to bulges and lumps, so try things on before you buy them. And choosing clothes which are too big adds to your size and makes you look fatter.

113. Choose items which can hide your problem areas. For instance, if you want to make your tummy look flatter, move away from skin tight vests, and choose a flattering tunic. Instead of choosing a mini skirt, hide chunky thighs under a float skirt.

114. If you have not fat on your body wear thongs and g-strings. But if you want to give the illusion of a skinny figure, go for supportive styles which help to pull in the tummy. A well fitting bra can also help to create a smoother slimmer figure.

115. Highlight your beautiful areas. If you have a

beautiful slender neck, but a bit of weight on your waistline, draw attention to your neck with an eye catching necklace, or other accessories. If you have toned arms, wear a sleeveless top to make the most of your assets.

116. Black is great as a quick fix as it is very slimming. So if you want to look skinny wear this color.

117. When buying pants, pay attention to the rise. Too high a rise can create the illusion of a tummy even if you have a 6-pack, and too low a rise can lead to belly pooch hanging over the top of your jeans which is not pretty.

118. It's very important to have a beautiful posture. Stand up straight, pull your stomach in, and your shoulders back. This is possibly the most important tip, as bad posture can add pounds visually.

LOOK YOUNGER AND FEEL BETTER TIPS

119. We all want to look young. Especially women. We spend endless dollars on surgical face lifts to bioxin treatments. There are some not so expensive methods, not so drastic for more youthful look.

120. It's very important to drink a lot of water. It's best to drink 8 glasses of water per day. Eat a healthy, nutritious diet, proper nutrition is key to looking your best and living a longer, healthy life.

121. Go often to a sauna. This helps the blood in your skin circulate better and brings all of the healthy nutrients to your face. You look better and younger. Saunas leave your skin super soft and you'll get an instant healthy glow.

122. Exercise a lot. Exercise to improve your shape and muscle tone. You can do it at your home or in a fitness center. It's really important to keep

your body in good shape because it's the key for health.

123. Look after your skin. Wrinkles are a major age giveaway. Use a good quality sun screen to protect your skin to ward off skin cancer.

124. Learn to have a positive, rather than negative attitude. The way you think, reflects on the way you look. Frowning causes wrinkles faster than smiling and makes you look less attractive.

GET TAN TIPS

125. Don't use a fake tanner because it makes everyone look orange. Go to a tanning booth. Be sure to take all the supplies with you, including tanning lotion/oil, goggles and perhaps a bathing suit or underwear. If it's your first time going to a tanning booth, don't go for very long; talk to the cashier about the recommended length.

126. It's expenisve to go to a tanning salon and spend a fortune on tanning. Home tanning is quite simple and can be very relaxing as well. Tan in your own backyard. Put on the smallest bathing suit or if the backyard is quite private you could even go topless.

127. Get a towel, some music, a magazine, sunglasses, a hat, a glass or bottle of water, and a friend. It will be really enjoyable for both of you and the more you keep yourself occupied, the longer you will want to stay out there.

128. It is very important to keep yourself hydrated, since you will be sweating out your body liquid. So don't forget to drink a lot of water.

Buy some SPF-15 tanning oil. This will promote a safe and healthy tan, without looking burnt. Never buy any without SPF. Whether you are tanning indoors in a tanning bed or enjoying the outdoors in the sunshine, always protect your eyes from exposure to UV light. UV light can permanently damage eyes and harm vision. So wear a hat and sunglasses that keep your head cool.

HAVE MANNER TIPS

129. Always think things out before you speak. If you talk without thinking you may say something that will make people laugh at you. Especially think before say if you are a person that may be poor at finding the right words to say.

130. Always use the terms "Thank You," and "You are Welcome" which will show that you have manners. People who lack manners do not use these terms.

131. Speak with respect for others. Never blame people. You can do this by avoiding negative remarks that may insult someone else, which should not be too hard to do.

132. There is one manner that has never changed. Always hold open a door for anyone following you closely. By doing this people will feel special and will respect you.

133. Pay attention to how you carry yourself. Your shoes should be clean, your hair should shine etc. Act like you have some class, which goes hand in hand with manners.

134. Never interrupt a person that is speaking and wait for him till he finish. Then you can start talking. An enormous lack of manners is when you interrupt people. This can be very annoying.

135. When you did not hear something that an individual has said, never use the word "What?" as it tends to come off as brash. Instead, use "Could you say that again for me, please?" or "I'm sorry?"

136. If someone else is speaking, try hard not to be domineering by taking over the story or subject matter at hand even if you feel that you know it better.

137. Don't eat while talking on the phone because making awful noises in someone's ear isn't nice and doesn't show good manners. And be sure to turn off your cell phone in movie, theaters, and don't drive with a cell phone stuck to your ear.

138. Good manners will never go out of style. So practice having good manners because they will be always modern and will help you a lot in the long run.

BE CONFIDENT TIPS

139. Hold your head high and don't look down. Make eye contact when you talk to someone. Always dress nice, because this will make you feel good and will raise your confidence.

140. Don't be shy. People don't like shy people. If you want to impress someone you can do it only when you show confidence. When you respect yourself, people will respect you. But if you act like you're inferior, people will think you are.

141. Be yourself and never fake. Don't try to pretend somebody you are not. Try not to compare yourself so much with other people, it is a wasteful pursuit and you could be doing something better.

142. Think of those confident, unique people that you wish you were more like. Someone close to you, or someone famous and think of the qualities, physical, emotional, moral, and spiritual, that the

role model displays and work towards acquiring those.

143. Celebrate the things that make you different. Remember that you are unique and no one can compare to you. If you know you've got something special or different, work it don't hide it.

144. When someone compliments you, remember what they've said, and when you're feeling insecure, just say to yourself, for example, "Mark loves my eyes". And really look at the quality that you've been complimented on. You can write down on a paper all your compliments and read it when you feel insecure. Whatever it takes to make you feel good before you hit the door for work in the morning – do it.

145. Stay active. Don't sit around doing absolutely nothing. Exercise, do a sport, dance, walk your dog, go shopping, just get out and enjoy. If you just stay at home that may bring you down.

146. Get creative with your memories. Watch often your pictures form your birthday or other occasion where you look stunning. You will remind what a hot woman you are and this will make you more confident.

147. Smile a lot. Even if you're not, act like you're happy. Show that you are bright and energetic

person and people will want to look like you. Even if it is not true, show others that you live in a pink world.

148. If you don't respect yourself, nobody else will. Don't put yourself down just because you think you're fat or skinny or the wrong shape etc. Value yourself because you are unique and different.

149. Try not to compare yourself so much with other people, it is a wasteful pursuit and you could be doing something better. Be glad of who you are. Always value yourself and you will see how people will adore you.

BE RESPECTED TIPS

150. Always be groomed and dressed neatly and present yourself as a clean person. Clothing doesn't need to be expensive but it should be laundered and in good repair. Keep your hair clean and take care of your teeth. Your ready smile will show others that you enjoy your own company and theirs too.

151. Your language should be clean and respectable. Never tell negative things about people but also don't flatter a lot because people can recognize the difference between true interest and forced compliments.

152. Your neighbors will respect you if you keep your home and surroundings clean and well kept. It will be a better place for everyone.

153. Don't act like you know it all. People do not appreciate it when you act superior to them. Don't try too hard, people won't respect you because they

will assume you are trying to be better than them.

154.   Set an example others would like to follow. When another person imitates you, it is a sign of respect. Appreciate it when someone else has set a good example.

155.   Give everyone a chance. Even if you realize someone is an idiot, always be civil and have class. People around you will respect that more than bad behaving confronting them in a mean way.

156.   Try to find what you're good at, and use it. Show your talents. This is a great way to get 'well-known'.

157.   Never bully others or take advantage of their weaknesses. Do not scream at the other person, or speak abusively. People don't respect bullies because they don't show respect. Allow people to keep their dignity.

158.   Some people may just want to pick a fight with someone, or engage in an argument. Recognize when this is the case, and walk away. There is no need to waste your time with such people.

BE KNOWN TO EVERYONE AS A KIND PERSON TIPS

159. Everyone wants a good reputation but it is difficult to obtain one. You have to earn it yourself. You'll have to be kind in every situation to get the best reputation. As you already know you should smile a lot to show people that you are open and willing to make friends.

160. When people give you compliments, show them that you appreciate that and always say thank you. You should also use compliments to make people comfortable with you. But don't go too far because people will think that your compliments are fake.

161. Be friendly with everyone. Try to imagine that they are all your friends and be nice with them. You want to be treated well, so do the same to all people.

162. Don't use dirty words and never be rude. Always be positive. Try never to get mad at anyone. If a person annoys you, don't let them know that. Be diplomatic.

163. Try to always be in a good mood. People don't like to listen about problems, sadness and other things that will ruin their great mood. Just be yourself but be nicer. Always laugh at their jokes, even if they're lame.

164. Always say your opinion, tell what you feel but never be mean about it. Listen. This is one of the main skills in life. It's a hard skill to learn, but you'll get the hang of it.

165. Be know as a hard worker and not a lazy person. Someone who is determined and cares about everyone, but can still crack a joke every now and then. Let people like you because of who you are.

166. Try to accept every invitation. If someone invites you to join them to a party it's good that you immediately accept. People won't like you if you always refuse their invitations. If you are desperate for friends and spend your time sitting alone, people may come to you, but only because they feel sorry for you.

IMPRESSION ON THE PHONE TIPS

167. It's great to have more likeable and confident telephone voice. First, take a photo of someone you love or something that inspires you and look at it. This will keep you constantly positive. And take a moment to let go of whatever you were working on so you can focus on the conversation. Try to smile before picking up the phone; it will make a difference in how you sound.

168. When you talk you should always smile because when we smile our voices naturally become warmer, brighter and friendlier.

169. If you are well dressed and you like yourself, your voice will sound very confident. If you want to talk to a man who you like, dress always nice and you will be impressed by your powerful and sexy voice.

170. You should always stand up when you talk on the phone, because this will generate energy in your body and your voice.

171. Speak slower. Especially if you are communicating with someone that may be fluent in a language or from a background different than your own.

172. Go to a quiet place, as not to disturb others with your talking, so you can hear more clearly. If you want to get off the phone, do it politely. You don't want to upset people by hanging up abruptly.

ARRIVE TO A PARTY LIKE A DIVA

173. If you take a taxi, make sure the driver drops you off around the corner. Someone from the party may see you exit. You always want to at least seem like you've arrived in style.

174. Never seem nervous or as if you are in a hurry. Be calm and confident. Always walk down the street and to the door as if you are on a fashion show runway.

175. Knock on the door or ring the bell very lightly and with grace. When the door is answered, respond as if you have nothing better to do.

176. Stand in the middle of the door frame. Stay there for a few seconds and give a slow glance across the room. Feel confident and sexy.

177. Go to the center of the room with a smooth glide. Remember to keep your head high. All

eyes are on you now.

178. Look around the room and give each person a shady or distant glance. Give a light kiss on the cheek of the first fierce person you see. Give a sexy smile until someone offers to take your coat or bag. That's it!

MAKE NEW FRIENDS TIPS

179. If you are around new place, try to find people who are not attached to a group and strike up a conversation about anything -- the weather, the environment you're in, clothes, and pets, whatever.

180. Make sure you are organized and not sloppy because when you are sloppy, people are not going to like the real you and they will judge you by the way you look and/or the things you have. Have confidence and don't slouch when you walk. Try to always have a fun time.

181. Mainly, just be yourself. If people don't like you when you're yourself, maybe you shouldn't be around them. Don't waste your time to make them like you, if you don't feel comfortable with them, then just leave them. There are better people who will like you the way you are.

182. It's very important to remember person's name.

Repeat the name several times to remember it. It's good next time when you see the person to know his/her name.

183. Remember, never leave old friends because you like someone else more. This is a mistake. And switching from one group of friends to another all the time will have unintended results.

184. Call your friends at least once a week to check on them and see how they're doing. They'll be happy you care. Tell them that you appreciate them. They will be glad that you think about them.

185. Be as loyal as a puppy to your friends, they'll respect you for it. Breaking a secret not only would lose your friend's trust, but the trust of everyone around you.

186. Accept everyone for who they are and never bring anyone down or try to change someone. If someone offends you then just ignore him.

187. Remember important things about them such as things they like and their birthdays.

188. Don't be afraid to stand up for what is right. If you know one of your friends is doing something that you know is wrong, confront them. If you're a friend, you won't let them do the wrong thing.

189.   Be sincerely interested in what others have to say. Look them in the eyes. Listen carefully. Ask questions. Empathize. Laugh. Be good company.

190.   An important tip for making friends is to never do things you do not like to do. This may cause you to lose one friend, but it will also give you a lot of friends for sticking up for the things that you like and the things you don't like.

191.   Be optimistic. Even if you are feeling really down, remember that there's always something out there to smile about. A positive outlook will make people want to be around you more. Everyone loves to communicate with happy, positive and smiling people.

192.   Crack a joke. Having a sense of humor is important, but don't get too carried away - you have to be serious about some things, sometimes. Telling a joke can easily break the ice and define your character and what you like to do.

193.   There are people around you who are funny and sociable. Analyze their behavior and see what they do. Identify their cues and attempt to assimilate some of their beneficial patterns into your demeanor.

194.   Always try to accept others' offers and invitations and be with them. Also make invitations to others;

it's a good way to show people you enjoy them and they'll like you for it.

195. Smiling is very important. Smile as much as you can. Signs of encouragement let people know you care about what they are saying.

196. Listen more rather than talking. Instead of nodding and smiling and occasionally wiping the drool off your face, try to take what the person says and run with it. He will be glad that you care about what he tells you and will appreciate that.

197. It's easier to talk to people if you have shared an experience with them. Clearly the friends you have at the moment predominantly talk about interesting things they did in the past.

198. The 'key thing' in a conversation is the word 'you'. Ask them about themselves. Don't go talking about yourself the whole time! If you notice you are saying "I" too much or are just talking about yourself, hurry up and finish that sentence and ask them about what they like.

199. Be comfortable with yourself and present a confident image, it will be much easier to have others see that and want to be around you. Once you are okay with being alone and happy with who you are, it'll be easier to make friends.

GREAT CONVERSATION TIPS

200. You will never be able to relax if you are too busy thinking about yourself, what you look like, or what the other person might be thinking. When you meet new people, talk mostly about them, people just love to talk about themselves.

201. You should find out what the other person is interested in. What does he like to do during his free time, his hobbies and other interests. You can even check in advance when you know you will have an opportunity to talk with a specific person. It's also good to start with a compliment. Everyone likes sincere compliments, and that can be a great ice-breaker.

202. You should always ask questions. What do they like to do? What did they do today or last weekend? What kind of music do they like? Ask questions about movies, sports, television programs, or other entertainment etc. Before going

to an event where you will be required to make conversation, read the day's news and brush-up on current entertainment news. This will provide some instant conversation subjects of current interest.

203.   It's not good to talk about yourself especially if you give them your life story. You are less likely to regret things you have said if you take a moment to come up with a more polite way to say it.

204.   Be a good listener and never disturb while the other person is talking. Show respect to the other person when you use your "speaking turn" to show you have been listening and not just to say something new.

205.   Be careful for taboo subjects. Watch for cues to determine if the subject is welcome. The subject seems to make the other person uncomfortable, simply drop it and move on without worry.

206.   Try not to argue. You do not have to agree with everything someone says, but you do not have to tell them all about how you disagree. It is better to simply change the subject in a casual conversation than to get involved in an argument.

DRESS FOR A FIRST DATE TIPS

207. Every relationship is based on a first impression. So try to look gorgeous. That doesn't mean to go out and buy a whole new wardrobe. Whatever you have hanging around in your closet should work just fine.

208. Don't be afraid to be different. You'll want to stand out from all the other girls or guys to catch your date's attention. Avoid black on a first date. Dress something colorful. As you remember the color which attracts guys is the pink-peach color. Women look very sweet and feminine in pink.

209. Be casual. You want to look nice, but don't try too hard. Friends will tell you if you look good or not and give you advice.

210. Don't be too cautious. Wear something that shows

off those muscles you worked for, your great tummy, don't be afraid to show a little skin.

211.   Keep your outfit simple and don't overdress for the occasion. If you're going out to see a movie, then maybe wear jeans or a skirt and a nice top. A colorful sexy top. Make sure you're comfortable and feel good about yourself and what you're wearing. The worst thing you can do is go out feeling ugly. All night you'll be self-conscious, and the date will be over before it starts.

FLIRT WITH A MAN TIPS

212. Look him in the eyes as a sign of affection and confidence. If he approaches you start a conversation, but don't make it too obvious that you like him.

213. Play with your hair or clothing. This look very appealing to men. Also, touch him whenever you can, on his arm or wherever else. Don't make it too obvious.

214. Once you've got his attention, look him in the eyes and smile. If he smiles back, slowly look down, and repeat. Guys like girls who can show off their smile. And as you already know you will look more beautiful when you smile.

215. Don't make it too obvious when he's around his friends, unless you know that he likes you. Laugh with him, and help him to feel comfortable around you. Break the ice together.

216.   Don't try to be someone you aren't. You attract the kind of person you are. Don't pretend to be somebody you are not.

217.   Try not to make it obvious that you are flirting and don't try too hard to impress him. Whenever he's around, make sure you're having fun so that he'll want to join in.

218.   Remember what he mentions in passing (it's the little things that count) and bring it up later as a question. For example, he says "I've got to go home, I'm helping my sister clean for her birthday tomorrow." Later, you ask, "Did your sister enjoy her birthday party?".

219.   Do your research. If he mentions that he loves basketball, ask him if he watched the game on the weekend, and know the score or something that happened so you can talk about it. If you don't know much about what he likes, get him to teach you something about it - he will feel knowledgeable and important, and it's the perfect excuse to spend time with him.

220.   If his friends don't like you and he keeps you a secret this just shows that he isn't proud of his woman and you want someone who wants you for you and doesn't care about what others think. You don't have to rush to say that you're in love or not; so don't trap him.

221.   Make sure he doesn't have a girlfriend who will be upset and resentful if you flirt with him. There is a possibility that he has a girlfriend but is not at the moment with him. He may lie that he is single, so never fall in love before you know him better. Otherwise, you may suffer a lot. You don't deserve that!

222.   Don't pretend to be interested in something just for the sake of flirting - if you decide to make a move, it might mean you end up pretending to be someone you're not. Let people like you the way you are. Be yourself. It's great feeling to be liked for who you are.

UNDERSTANDING MEN TIPS

223. Most women don't understand men and this can affect their relationship. It's important to always have a lot of money and show him that you are an independent woman who doesn't need his money. Men will make a great impression on a woman about their finances early in the relationship, only for her to find out later that the money isn't what it seems.

224. Be patient with your man. Let him enjoy his hobbies, like sports. Give him enough time to spend with his friends, drink beer and watch the game on the TV. If you want to rub him the wrong way real fast, talk to him while a game is on or tie up his day shopping when the game is about to start and you may find yourself without a man.

225. Get physical. Be closer with him. Most men have this desire to be playfully physical with you, each other or by themselves. For example, shadow

boxing, wrestling, shoving, running or simply clicking the remote. Some men still haven't grown up and will enjoy making you a part of their playfulness for instance, pulling hair, slapping a butt, streaking, etc.

226. Be careful how you dress. Sexy attire to men spells sex. If you are wearing a mini-skirt and your breasts are protruding out, it is hard for a man to think about anything else. If you aren't interested in sex, don't give him the wrong impression.

227. Prepare yourself for a double standard when it comes to looks. Most men after have gotten to know you stop care for their looks. They begin not to care about their pot bellies (yet they will criticize a woman for being overweight), lose their hair and aren't mindful of their breath. So be prepared of such things.

228. Become friend with his friends. Accept his other female friends and acquaintances. Many men do a lot of talking with at least one female whether in the family or someone on the job. Don't be jealous. When he bought jewelry, clothes or some other gift for you, the woman on the job or the female relative more than likely was the one he consulted with before he made the purchase. There are a few men out there who just won't talk to any woman other than his wife or girlfriend about any personal issues, but those men are hard to find.

SEDUCE MEN TIPS

229. Imagine walking into a room or down the street, knowing that you look sophisticated, confident, and self-assured...and that men everywhere are gazing at you in admiration, longing to get to know you. We all want to be an object of desire- the kind of woman that men talk about, dream about and long to be with. We all want to be chased and admired by men and to be appreciated, respected and admired for our existence, appearance, personality and accomplishments. It's very important to look your best, because you never know where or when you are going to meet someone. Put lipstick and comb your hair even if you go to the gym. Wear attractive clothes and accessories. The best color for clothes is pink-peach which most attracts men. That color is flattering to most skin tones.

230. Dress fashionably but that doesn't mean to wear expensive clothing. Expensive clothes are not the

most important thing to a man, but it is important that a woman keep up with her appearance. So keep yourself well groomed and be updated with fashion. When you dress it's good to live something for the imagination. Always dress sexy, but classy.

231. It's important to express intellect, because it's not enough to have just pretty face and perfect body. A man would like to have a woman with who to talk something about, who will teach him new things, just as well he will teach you new things. Share your hobbies and tell him the most interesting things that have happened to you and show what he has been missing out on before he met you.

232. It's crucial to love your body, because men love woman who loves her body. A woman who finds her body sexy and walks around feeling very beautiful is incredibly desired to a man and make him curious and eager to get to know that woman. When you like your body and feel comfortable with it, people will feel your confidence and will also like it. Remember that nobody is perfect-everyone has defects, but that does not mean that you should advertise your defects.

233. Flirt with him by sending silent signals of your interest through subtle body language. Body language is everything. If a man is standing across the room and you are interested in him, tilt your

head, drop your eyes, and then look back at him, give your hair a slight flip and stroke the inside of your arm or your neck. By doing this you will let him know that you would be interested in talking to him.

234. Let him know you're different from all the rest. Emphasize your originality through your appearance, personality, intelligence and behavior. Don't try to pretend that you're anyone other than yourself. It is easy to sense a real person from an artificial one and one of the main turn offs for a man is a woman who is not herself and gives off a fake vibe.

235. Make him feel like he's the most important person in the world by focusing your full attention on him. Listen intently to what he has to say, and respond with respect for his opinions.

236. Give him a reason to think about you. Wear a lingering fragrance that haunts his memory, soft clothes that he yearns to touch, and a smile that he can't get out of his mind.

237. Be sincere and friendly, compliment him the way you would want to be complimented. Compliment him on the situation at hand. For example, tell him he has some great skills on the dance floor.

238. Mention that he has a nice smile - but don't be

lecherous. Simply say, "You've got a nice smile." Note an article of his outfit that catches your eye: "Great frames!" "Cool sweater!"

239. Create an opportunity to be alone together - nothing as serious as dinner, because if the evening doesn't go as planned, you will have to sit through the entire meal wondering why you let yourself get into this situation.

240. Be engaging. A woman who is sitting with a bunch of men is intriguing. Those guys are sitting with her for a reason. Other men will want to know what it is.

241. Ask the man about his work, his hobbies and his interests. Listen carefully and ask questions. Find out what he's interested in. If you can hold your own in a discussion on baseball, stock cars or fishing, you're in.

242. Don't drink too much. Your inhibitions will be lowered and you might say or do things you wouldn't normally do.

243. Never lose your special feminine roots- show him your sweet and romantic side. Today women are more independent and career oriented, but that does not mean we should have to give up and forget our feminine roots. So show him how sweet and care taking you are.

244. When you're talking to him, focus all your attention on him, talk only to him, and treat him like he is the only thing you care about. However, suddenly draw your attention back and ignore him. Go to another room, talk to other people, and get involved in a game. Later, return to the man and once again focus all of your attention on him. By giving the man all your attention he feels really special and he feels really good to be around you. Then, when you draw your attention away, it makes him miss you, which makes him want to be around you even more. It also makes him think you're a cool woman by being really social and fun, instead of some needy loser who only wants to be around him.

KNOW IF HE IS THE ONE TIPS

245. See if you naturally remember his birthday, your anniversary, and days that are important to him. If you don't remember such important days then obviously you don't care much for him.

246. Notice if you tell your friends/family how great he is and if you are excited to introduce him to them. If you care you will include him in family plans, such as inviting him to a family dinner or help him get along with his family, even sticking up for him, because it is important to you that his family like you and you like them.

247. Pay attention if you openly tell him that you love him. Do you really mean it when you say it? If when you say "I love you tons and tons and tons," he hesitantly replies "Yeah, I love you too," he probably doesn't feel as strongly for you as you do for him.

248. See if you want to talk with him about your future. See if you really want your relationship to last forever. Ask yourself "Can I live without him?" If he won't discuss your future together, even after a significant amount of time together (say a year), he is probably not considering a future.

249. If he refuses to include you, at least occasionally, in his plans with the boys or avoids telling you what he and the boys did last night, then he is probably doing something you wouldn't approve of.

250. See if you want to give him a key to your apartment/house and/or you make a point of telling him that you have never given this key out to any other boyfriend. Express how important it is to you that he feels comfortable in your house.

251. Be sure that you feel comfortable with him seeing you without make-up, without your hair done or after a sweaty workout. Make sure that you feel comfortable using his bathroom.

252. Check if the man is a guy who is overly controlling. May be he is insecure and feels that he has the upper hand in your relationship. If he frequently tells you what to do or tries to run your life, stay away from him. He is not "The One", because "The One" will be secure with you and let you be who you are.

BE A RULES GIRL AND GET THE MAN YOU WANT TIPS

253.   Realize that you are a creature unlike any other. Feel unique and special. One of a kind. If you feel this way about yourself, men will see you that way. Take time to make yourself look the best you possibly can on the outside to make yourself feel confident on the inside. Confident girls are attractive to men.

254.   You should never- make the first move, ask him out and call him first. No matter what, there are no exceptions to this rule. All men, whether they know it or not, are programmed to pursue and will appreciate it in the end if you do not make the first move.

255.   You do not want to be an open book now do you? So be mysterious. Answer his questions truthfully but do not start talking about your family problems

on the first few dates. Men do not need to know everything about you, especially not right away.

256. Wait a while to sleep with him. Nothing more than kissing on the first three dates. He is not so irresistible so you can wait a bit. This will earn his respect.

257. Be independent. Show him that you got it all and you don't need his money. Show him that you can live terrific life without having him. He is your boyfriend and you need to maintain your other relationships and interests. A guy should always add to your life, not take away from it.

258. Let him pursue you. Do not talk on the phone with him for longer than ten minutes. Set a timer if you have to. This way you will remain mysterious when you tell him that it was nice talking to him but you are just so busy. Don't call a man either. He should call you five times for every one time you call him. If he's interested in you, he will keep calling.

259. Don't get hung up on one guy. If you think only for one man, it's very possible for you to fall in love in him. So flirt with other guys. If he doesn't ask you out, he's not interested and it was never meant to be. Accept it and move on. May be he will ask you out then or maybe he won't. There is someone else out there for you.

260. You may have noticed how there are so many guys you could have that you just aren't interested in but the one you do like shows no interest back. This is because you unknowingly do the rules on the men you don't like. You don't call them excessively, you don't act interested.

261. Remember that revealing your feelings to a man and acting clingy when he doesn't like you will drive your chances of being with him to a zero. Don't do it because you will just embarrass yourself and get hurt. By following the rules you do not get hurt because you do not pursue and you know that if a guy doesn't call you it isn't because you called too much or saw him too much. It will be because it wasn't meant to be.

MAKE HIM PAY MORE ATTENTION TO YOU AND NOT HIS FRIENDS TIPS

262. Be independent. Make sure you have your own interests and friends, if he goes out with his friends then go out with yours and hang around. Also, don't let him hold you back from your hobbies. For example, if you like to ride a horse, do it. He will love the fact that you are an independent woman who has her own interests. He will know that even without him, you can have a great time.

263. Care about yourself. Do what you want to do, don't spend time worrying over how you look in the mirror. Don't let "looking good" make you obsessed of it. If he's going out with you for your looks, he probably wants your body more than your heart.

264. Be yourself around him and try to have conversation with him and his friends. You can talk and joke with them. Just make yourself part of his circle of friends. He will be very glad if his friends like you.

265. You may be his girlfriend but you are also his friend. So be sure to be there for him when he needs it most, and he should be there for you, too.

266. Don't worry too much about changing him. Remember you were drawn to the man before you were dating. If something needs tweaking do a little behavior modification. Show him by being a role model.

267. When you are going out with your boyfriend, don't always expect him to always come up with the date plan. Add your own input. Take him to places that he has never been before.

268. Don't mind when your boyfriend has a "night out with the guys". Show him that you trust him and he will appreciate it.

MAKE HIM CHASE YOU TIPS

269.   Seduce his mind first. You must get in his head and have him thinking about you. You must make him feel comfortable with you. Make him can't stop thinking about you.

270.   Listen and talk to him. Men feel closer to you if you listen and remember what you talked about. In a way, words are a form of intercourse for a man because it's the only thing they have with which to establish trust with you. Find out his likes and dislikes, his needs and desires. Laugh with him and agree with him when you can.

271.   Take things slowly. Show him that you're patient; your ability to resist him will make him wonder if you're really interested, and will motivate him to show you that he's worth being interested in.

272.   Kiss with your eyes first. Men need to feel a connection with you. You begin this connection

through your words and then your eyes. If you can keep his eyes on yours, and hypnotize him with your words, you are halfway there. So keep him watching and seduce him with your sexy eyes.

273. Talk about sex or sexy things. At some point, begin to talk about sex...not between the two of you, but general experiences you've had. Once you inject the topic of sex, it will be on their mind when they think about you. Talking about the act makes them more comfortable with the act.

274. Men put a lot of stock in what their friends think of prospective suitors. If you want to date a particular man, demonstrate your good qualities (e.g., sense of humor, good taste, charitable nature) around his friends.

275. Talk to him frequently. The best approach is email or chat. It gives you direct access to his head because you can be as intimate as you want and he can mull your words while you are not around.

276. Don't become too caught up in saying the right thing and all that...the most important thing is to socialize with men. If you enjoy yourself, the rest should just follow...so don't be too uptight.

277. Do not try so hard for him to notice you. If you are laughing and having a good time rather than

always looking in his direction then you will have a better chance.

278. Learn to dance. Dancing is one of the most seductive things a woman can do. Seduction works on the brain. It's the art against his will. If he is attracted to you at first, that doesn't count as a seduction and you need more practice.

279. Ignore him for a little while. Never reveal too much of yourself because you almost certainly will turn him off.

280. Never call first. Be patient. Lately there's a lot of self help advice going around that tells guys not to call a woman for anywhere between 2 days to 2 weeks after first meeting and getting the phone number. When you feel you've waited long enough, be that 2 days or a week, send out a probe. One sms, call, or message is enough. You're just checking to see if he's alive, and that is all.

SUPPORT YOUR MAN TIPS

281. Everyone wants to be supported and needs it at points in their life. Supporting your man is key in a relationship. Men need support the most. You should be always there for your man. He has to be sure about that. Make sure that when he has been through something stressful, you ask him first, don't be egoistic and wait for them to hint you to ask them.

282. Men want to know that you really care. Be a good listener. Don't fidget or switch the topic right away, let them know that you're going to listen to everything they have to say. Pay attention to their body language. Men tend to keep some things underwrap.

283. When you see that he is down kiss and hug him and make sure they have some support, so they'll come to you again next time. Show that you're understanding and not give them attitude after.

284. Tell him that it's okay, and it happens, and you can get through this together. Make your guy feel respected and let him know that you want the same in return.

285. There is always give and take in a relationship just make sure that it is semi equal and don't let the guy take advantage of your support.

GAY FRIENDS TIPS

286.   It's nice to have a gay friend. They support, amuse, and accompany their straight girlfriends everywhere. Begin to look for a gay. Look around your job, clubs, anywhere. If you don't find gay friend in such places grab some of your fabulous girlfriends and head to a gay bar for a night of dancing. Luckily, three in one hundred men are gay, so you have plenty of chances.

287.   Don't forget that gay men are as diverse as all the men in the world. They come from every ethnic group, religion, and culture. They are not animals, and they can smell desperation. Be friendly, clever, attractive, and a real friend. If you want someone to cry about your boyfriend, you have to be there for him to cry too.

288.   Don't assume your gay friend will want to do "girl things" with you. Gay men are still men. Gay men are not women. They are men, and will

occasionally be just as confused by your girlish ways as any straight man.

289. When you go out to a gay bar go out and dance. Because gay men want to date men doesn't mean that gay men won't dance with a woman who knows how to have a good time. After the dance go to the bar, take drinks, start conversation and introduce your friends to each other.

290. Do not fall in love- a gay friend is not waiting for the right girl. He likes boys. Deal with it. Getting your heart involved is dangerous- you will get hurt and it's not fair when you know he's gay from the beginning. He's not gay to hurt your feelings. It's just the way he is.

291. Don't forget to go to a straight bar occasionally. Gay friends are lovely, but there is no reason to give up on being a sexual creature yourself. So go to other places too. Or you can take your new gay friend to the places where you like to go.

292. If you find a straight boyfriend don't dump your gay friend. Stay friend with him and continue to go out and have fun with him. If you expect your friends to stick by you, they should still be your friends even when you're in a relationship. And if your straight boyfriend gets jealous, think about whether he's right for you. May be he is very possessive which is not right.

IS HE CHEATING TIPS

293. If you seriously suspect that your man is cheating there are several ways to find out if this is true. If he is unfaithful he will be more attentive to your needs than usual. He will feel guilty in the early stages of his affair. The attention will disappear as the affair continues.

294. Your man will start to buy you gifts. Very expensive gifts-lots of gifts. He will feel guilty about betraying you and showering you with presents makes him feel better.

295. If you begin to think something is wrong, then you may be right. So pay attention to your instincts. Ignoring them means you want to blind yourself to the truth.

296. If he starts to fight with you often, then may be he looks for a reason to get mad and storm out of the house and thus the opportunity to meet a lover.

297. Be suspicious if he constantly talks about your relationship ending when you fight or argue. If he tells negative things about your relationship like "What would you do if our relationship ended?" Your man makes these statements because he has a lover to fall back on if your relationship ends.

298. If he acts depressed when he is around you and excited when leaving. If your man is in long-term affair, he will try to keep both relationships running smoothly. Any problems the cheater has in one relationship will spill over into the other relationship as well. This is unavoidable.

299. If he has become very cold and doesn't talk to you. If you live together but don't interact. This is another sign that he cheats on you.

300. If your man's cellphone is off (or voicemail on) a bit too much when you call lately.

301. If he is suddenly obsessed with his looks. If he changes his clothes, underwear, or hairstyle.

302. If he becomes secretive about his email and internet passwords.

303. When you two are having a lot less sex than usual.

304. If your man's taste in movies, music, or politics has mysteriously changed.

305. If he tells jokes or express opinions that are unusual for him.

306. If he talks in his dream and mention a name of a woman more than one occasion.

307. Your man behavior is such that your friends begin asking you what's wrong. When people notice tension or discord between the two of you before you are fully aware of it.

GET OVER A BREAK UP TIPS

308. First of all, you should be sure that it is not only your fault. It takes two people to make a relationship start, and one discordant person is enough to have it break up.

309. Accept your pain and cry as much as you want. It's okay to be hurt and feel alone and feel like you have messed up. But you have to know that you are a good person and this is not all one-sided.

310. Keep distance with him. It's not good to see him anymore because this way you won't be able to forget him. No phone calls, no e-mails, no IMing, and most importantly, no sex!

311. You can think about why you two have broken but never blame yourself. There had to have been a reason for it all to end, right? If there was a reason but it wasn't a good one, then this person isn't worth your time.

312. It's normal to be angry and furious. The amount of anger you feel all depends on how bad the "split" was. You may even begin to hate yourself. Don't do that get out of that feeling fast. It's a waste of time to be hating and ripping yourself apart for no reason.

313. Talk with your closest friends. They will always advise you and help. When you feel down, talk a lot with your friends about him. You can even cry in front of them.

314. Write all your feelings down. You can even write poems. One of the best results of writing it all down is that sometimes you will be amazed by a sudden insight that comes to you as you are pouring out your thoughts onto paper. This will help you to over come your pain. Just because it didn't work out doesn't mean it wasn't a necessary part of your journey to becoming who you're meant to be.

315. Keep only fond memories. Think about the good moments and be glad that you have had such a lovely moments. But never regret that they are over, because there will be new, more exciting emotions with a new better guy.

316. You may be feeling lonely, and want to be with someone. There is nothing as tacky from jumping from relationship to relationship as a leech jumps

from host to host. Although you may think you truly like another person soon after your first love, most likely you are just subconsciously afraid of being alone.

317.   Try to avoid friends who are very close with your ex, or common friends. Erase his number from your phone. This will aid you in avoiding the late-night drunk-dials, unless you have a knack for remembering phone numbers.

318.   Although you may be tempted to take revenge, or send notification through your friends about your great success in life without them -- don't exert the energy. Allow God to take care of everything on its own.

MAKE THE EX JEALOUS TIPS

319. If you want to make him regret breaking up with you there are some surefire methods. When your ex is near, start to flirt subtly with a guy you know. Just look this guy in the eyes and focus your attention on him while you talk. It should look that you really enjoy his company and that you are very interested in talking to him. You should be relaxed and friendly. Look happy and smile a lot.

320. If your ex tries to talk to you, be friendly but give him typical answers. Don't engage too much in the conversation and give short answers. Act as if you're over it. Even if it's not completely true.

321. The most important thing is to keep an eye contact with him to a minimum. It's going to burn him up. Don't stop to have fun and enjoy your time. Talk to people, laugh and demonstrate that you have a lovely time. Be confident and of course look your best.

WHEN A GIRL WANTS TO STEAL YOUR BOYFRIEND TIPS

322. If a girl who has never wanted to hang with you suddenly starts to hang out with you, it most likely she wants something from you. And most likely she wants your new boyfriend. Hang around her less.

323. If this doesn't work and she is still cheeky, tell her that you feel uncomfortable. Tell her that you need space and want to hang only with your boyfriend. In other words, tell her to back off.

324. If she hangs around your guy, tell her to back off if you have not already. If you have, tell your guy what you think she is doing. Always tell him what you think.

325. She may have had a plan from the start to ruin your relationship. She might have even told you

that he was flirting with her. But, if that is the case and you know that your boyfriend wouldn't lie to you, she is lying. But if you don't trust your boyfriend then test him. Before that, think if it's worthy to go out with a man without having trust in him.

326. Tell this girl off in front of a lot of people, if she says something back get your friends and your boyfriend to defend you. If she try to insult you, your boyfriend will make her regret about what she has said and will tell her to leave and never come back.

327. If you have never met this girl, when you do, look at the way she acts around him. See if she touches him a lot, looks him in the eyes, flirts, or pays him more attention to him than to anyone else. Tell him that you don't like how she acts and if he cares about you he will send her off.

328. You can try to confront her, but chances are if she knew your boyfriend was committed and flirted with him anyway, she probably doesn't care what you have to say. Just stay close to him and don't allow others to flirt with him.

329. If he was dumb enough to cheat on you, let her have him. They deserve each other. But if he cheats on you, he will do the same to her. Such people are miserable and never happy. Be glad that

you have found out what a crap he is. He doesn't deserve your attention. You can also tell her that you are making her a gift, because you don't want him anymore.

330. If this girl is the girlfriend of one of his friends, there is the possibility that she is trying to use him to make her boyfriend jealous, or trying to use her boyfriend to get to yours. Some girls are crafty like this. There are girls everywhere who attract men this way. You are not the only girl who has been through this situation. Always expect the unexpected.

331. If you trust your boyfriend, try not to get into a fight with him for hanging out with this girl. Tell him you do trust him, but you noticed that this girl may be getting a little too flirty. Let him know that it bothers you, and leave it at that.

GET A MAN WHO HAS NO INTEREST IN RELATIONSHIP TIPS

332. First of all, consider why you want the man to like you. Is it just because he's attractive or because he is rich? If that's the reason you want him to like you, then you're probably going down a very difficult road. An attractive and rich man has probably had lots of girls approach him just for his looks. Having that kind of constant, shallow attention can leave a person feeling isolated, lonely, and misunderstood. It can also leave him doubting his own self-worth if that's the only reason he's approached. Step back a bit and reevaluate what you're looking for. It's unkind to go out with someone just to have a handsome or rich man on your arm.

333. A person who has no interest in relationships of

any kind is someone who's been hurt. Don't push them and don't use the word "relationship" or the phrase "getting closer". You need a strong friendship before a hurt person can open up. Another reason is that the person might want to be single and go out with many women instead of commiting to one. He probably wants to be free and have fun without any obligations. So if you want to have a relationship with this kind of a man you should prepare to be patient because it will be too difficult.

334. Rethink how you're approaching this. The phrase "get a man to" is manipulative. You can't force someone to like you. There are some people that just don't get along, friends or otherwise. You need to recognize that and look for people that you can develop real relationships with that are two-sided and not manipulative. But if you are in love and really want to get a man who has no interest in relationships than develop yourself as a person. Your talents, interests, and good nature, will make you more attractive. For example, buy something that he can't afford (brand new high class car or something that everyone will be impressed of). Go to an audition for an actress. It may be not a casting for a big movie but for a soap opera for instance. It's possible you win the role and who doesn't want to date a famous woman? Or try to host a TV show. Just think of something big to impress him. Show that you are independent

woman and that he will only miss if he does not want to have a relationship with you. So try to impress him and show that you are different from all other women.

335. Make sure that it is known that you don't want a relationship either, or care that he does not want one. The easiest way to make a person want something more is by making it impossible to obtain. So when he says he doesn't date, don't dwell on this but move on and say who cares.

336. It's possible that he may want to sleep with you and doesn't want to be your boyfriend. Let him know that you are a serious woman and that he can only have you if he is serious too. Show him that you are not easy. You are a woman with principles, a woman who knows what she wants. Be impossible to get for him. That might change his mind and become your boyfriend.

337. Show him what you have to offer in terms of friendship. Friendships are the basis of good relationships. If you have similar interests, talk about those. Talk about his interests, activities, etc., but keep it casual at first.

338. You may get to a point where you are almost in "a relationship," but refuse to put a title to it. You must continue to act like you are not in a relationship, for instance while being very nice

also flirting, or talking about other men. This way you further bring the man into the relationship by making him wonder what it would be like if you actually were in a relationship. The key is to make yourself seem like you do not care- providing too much attention is a sure-fire way to get the entire goal to backfire.

339. Never get into a relationship where you don't have a relationship but you act like there is. You'll probably end up getting hurt by the manipulative/destructive man you are pursuing. Chances are if he does not want a relationship he will act in ways that are destructive at times.

9 781432 703929